"A galaxy divided by war...

...peaceful worlds must choose sides...

STAR WARS

THE CLONE WARS™

THE VISUAL GUIDE

written by Jason Fry

CONTENTS

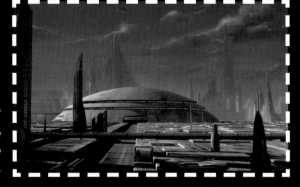

The Galactic Senate is the highest elected body of the Republic, now darkened by the growing stain of corruption.

Clone troopers were born and raised to serve the Republic and now defend its planets against a massive droid army.

The Republic Supreme Chancel committed thousand to the war aga Separatist Alliance. As the galaxy is divided efforts of the Jedi fracturing Republic is at war!.

r Palpatine has

of clone troopers

st Count Dooku's

planets choose sides,

and only the valiant

generals hold the

from tearing apart.

Supreme Chancellor Palpatine commands the Republic's armies and, through the Senate, the loyalty of the Jedi.

Count Dooku now leads the Separatists, but secretly takes orders from a hidden Master.

Jedi generals lead clone forces into battle on countless worlds.

REPUBLIC

THE REPUBLIC NAVY

For centuries, task forces commanded by individual star systems defended the Republic, but now a new centralized Navy fights the Separatists. This new starfleet is made up primarily of *Venator*-class Star Destroyers, nicknamed Jedi Cruisers, packed with fighters, assault ships, and AT-TEs.

JEDI CRUISER
RESOLUTE

CLONE TROOPER

SUPREME
CHANCELLOR

JEDI COUNCIL
Yoda, Mace Windu

JEDI GENERALS
Obi-Wan Kenobi, Anakin Skywalker

OFFICERS
Yularen, Wolffe

SPECIALIST TROOPERS
Rex, Cody, Gree, Fox

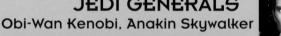

CLONE TROOPERS

THE JEDI KNIGHTS and clone troopers are the most visible Republic forces—and the symbols of a wartime bargain. The Jedi have defended the Republic for generations, but they are too few to defeat the Separatist threat. So the Jedi serve as generals in the Republic's Grand Army, made up of millions of clones. Under emergency powers granted by the Senate, the Supreme Chancellor commands the Jedi and the military.

BOUNTY HUNTERS

Loyal to neither side, galactic mercenaries like Cad Bane are in it for the credits, working for whoever pays the best.

SEPARATIST

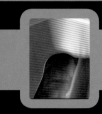

SITH LORD

PUBLIC LEADER
Count Dooku

SUPREME COMMANDER
General Grievous

SEPARATIST COMMANDERS
Asajj Ventress

SEPARATIST COUNCIL
Nute Gunray, Wat Tambor

DROID ARMIES

GRIEVOUS'S
FLAGSHIP
MALEVOLENCE

THE SEPARATIST FLEET

Banking Clan frigates, Trade
Federation battleships and
Commerce Guild destroyers make
up the bulk of the Separatist fleet—
but no vessel is as mighty as the
Malevolence, the massive flagship
commanded by General Grievous.

SUPER BATTLE
DROID

THE SEPARATISTS ARE formally known as the Confederacy
of Independent Systems (CIS), a movement dominated
by trade groups and giant corporations angry about
corruption in the Senate and greedy for more business.
The Separatists are publicly led by Count Dooku, who
commands fleets and droid armies contributed by
the member worlds and groups.

ANAKIN SKYWALKER

THE JEDI KNIGHT Anakin Skywalker is the greatest hero of a Republic at war and has proved his bravery on many battlefields. Yet his mentors Obi-Wan Kenobi and Yoda also see Anakin's recklessness. They worry that one day he will hurl himself into dangers from which even his uncanny ability with the Force will not be enough to save him.

RELUCTANT TEACHER

Anakin always said a Padawan would only slow him down. So when Ahsoka Tano turns up on Christophsis, he wants nothing to do with her. But Ahsoka's bravery and determination under Separatist fire win him over—and perhaps she reminds Anakin a bit of himself. "You're reckless," he tells her. "You never would have made it as Obi-Wan's Padawan—but you might make it as mine."

MECHANICAL HAND

THE HERO WITH NO FEAR

The Jedi say the Force is used for knowledge, and never for attack. But to Anakin, a Jedi on the offensive has no better ally than the Force.

THE WEAPON OF A JEDI KNIGHT

ARMORED CHEST PLATE

A JEDI'S SECRET

The Jedi are taught to avoid emotional attachments and relationships for fear of what they can unleash: The Jedi Code holds that fear, jealousy, greed, and anger are paths to the dark side of the Force. None of the Jedi know that Anakin has violated his vow of emotional detachment by marrying Padmé Amidala, the Senator from Naboo.

GENERAL SKYWALKER

★ Anakin's bravery is matched by the clone soldiers of the 501st Legion, led by the veteran Captain Rex. Though bred for loyalty, the clone troops have come to trust that their general will always find a path that leads to victory.

INTO BATTLE

Anakin and his clone troopers are ordered to save Jabba the Hutt's son from captivity and so they must storm a lofty castle on Teth. It's the perfect opportunity for Anakin to test his new Padawan—and himself—by doing what he loves best: Filling himself with the adrenaline of battle and the joy of feeling united with the wild power of the Force.

AHSOKA TANO

YOUNG AHSOKA TANO first meets her new Master, Anakin Skywalker, on the planet Christophsis. Anakin soon learns not to judge the little Togruta Padawan by her size—she proves resourceful and fearless despite little exposure to war. Soon a real bond has formed between "Skyguy" and "Snips"—a relationship that will be tested by the savagery of the Clone Wars.

BLUE LEADER

Ahsoka is a capable pilot, but there's a difference between skill behind the stick of a Jedi starfighter and skill leading men into battle. At Ryloth, Ahsoka commands her first squadron and finds her pilots are depending on her with their lives. The lesson she learns as Blue Leader will be important to her growth as both a Jedi and a commander.

BLADE EMITTER

JEDI IN TRAINING

Enthusiasm? Moxie? Ahsoka has these qualities in spades, but she knows that she lacks something crucial to becoming a Jedi Knight: Experience. There's no better place to acquire that than on the front lines of a galaxy at war—and at the side of Jedi such as Anakin, Luminara Unduli, and Plo Koon.

TOGRUTAS

☆ Togrutas are native to the planet Shili. Their colorful skins evolved as camouflage to confuse prey. Togrutas have two hollow montrals growing from the top of the skull and "head-tails" that fall over the chest and back. Ahsoka's montrals and head-tails haven't reached their adult length.

A NEW WARRIOR

Togrutas preserve their species' traditions as Jedi, including wearing trophies and elaborate costumes. As a young Togruta, Ahsoka's outfit is much more basic.

IMMATURE MONTRALS

GROWING HEAD-TAILS

EMERALD BLADE

TOGRUTA SASH

BATTLING GRIEVOUS

On Skytop Station, Ahsoka blocks Grievous's blade, which had been aimed at Captain Rex. The young Jedi Padawan then stands face to face with one of the Republic's mightiest foes.

PLO'S DISCOVERY

The Kel Dor Jedi Master Plo Koon first encountered Ahsoka Tano while he was on a mission to Shili. Plo brought the Force-sensitive baby back to the Jedi Temple on Coruscant to begin her training. Fourteen years later, their bond remains strong. While Plo wasn't considered as a Master for Ahsoka for fear of encouraging attachment, he is always pleased to see "Little 'Soka."

JEDI TRAINING

THE JEDI ARE servants of the galaxy. They are chosen as infants and rise through the Jedi Order as they grow in skill and feel for the Force.

JEDI MASTER

A Jedi Knight who trains a Padawan to knighthood becomes a Jedi Master, and may then take a new apprentice.

Promising initiates may be assigned to a Jedi for further training and to prove their worth to the Order. The relationship between Master and Padawan is an intense one. Both must learn about service and responsibility.

JEDI KNIGHT

Padawans judged worthy must pass the Trials. If they succeed, their Padawan braid is severed and they earn the rank of Jedi Knight.

JEDI COUNCIL

Twelve Jedi Masters direct the Jedi Order's affairs from atop the central spire of the Jedi Temple on Coruscant. There, they seek to divine the will of the Force and determine how best to serve the galaxy.

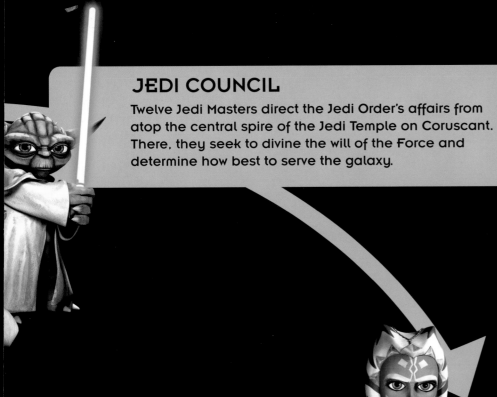

PADAWAN

Once chosen for the Jedi Order, younglings become Padawan apprentices, serving a Knight or Master.

YOUNGLINGS

Force-sensitive children are taken by the Jedi Order and trained communally to use the Force. Those chosen for further advancement become Padawans. Those not selected as apprentices are assigned to the Service Corps.

THE LOST TWENTY

Jedi lore has it that only 20 Jedi Masters have ever renounced the Order. Their departures are felt keenly by the Jedi, who memorialize them with busts in the Temple Archives. Count Dooku is the most recent of the Lost.

ASTROMECH AIRBORNE

R2-D2 is equipped with rocket thrusters, manufactured by Brooks Propulsion Devices. His thrusters let him fly to places his treads can't go, such as a distant landing platform on Teth. But while R2 enjoys flying, his BPD thrusters are a mixed blessing: They burn fuel quickly and the turbines are easily misaligned or damaged.

R2-D2

COURAGEOUS, LOYAL, STUBBORN, spirited, quirky—there's never been an astromech quite like R2-D2. Originally the property of the Royal House of Naboo, R2 serves Anakin during the Clone Wars. Only very rarely have a living being and a droid been so well-matched. Anakin sees R2 as a friend, and has rewarded the droid's loyalty by refusing to wipe his memory.

THE LITTLEST BATTLE DROID

R2-D2 isn't designed for combat, but he can control a starship's cannons. Sometimes his feisty nature leads him into altercations—where his electric prods and other tools make him a tough opponent. And there are other ways to fight: His holoprojector and audio-visual systems can distract, blind, or deafen an enemy.

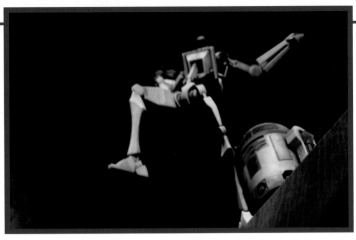

TOUGH FIGHTER

R2 is not afraid to get "pushy" when it comes to fighting battle droids.

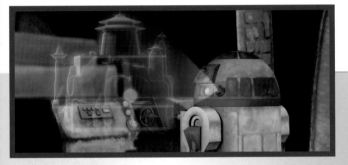

SCOUTING

R2's holoprojector can play back visuals or work with his auditory sensors to make 3-D models.

COMPUTER INTERFACE

R2 can communicate with most computer systems, find hidden files, and break codes.

BACKSEAT DRIVER

☆ When inserted into a starfighter's droid socket, astromechs like R2 make a star pilot's life much easier. They monitor flight performance, fix technical problems, boost power levels, target enemies, and aid navigation.

LOGIC FUNCTION
DISPLAY

SPACECRAFT
LINKAGE
AND
CONTROL
ARMS

BENEATH THE DOME

R2 normally keeps his chassis tightly sealed, but can open panels to reveal a number of arms, probes, and other tools.

PRIMARY
HOLO
PROJECTOR

RECHARGE
POWER
COUPLING

POWERBUS
CABLES

THE NEGOTIATOR

Obi-Wan is renowned throughout the galaxy as the Jedi's best negotiator, seemingly at ease among diplomats, warlords, and space pirates alike. Obi-Wan is a deadly warrior, but not a man of war. He has seen his fill of death and will always choose to spare his enemies' lives if they truly accept peace.

OBI-WAN KENOBI

OBI-WAN IS A skilled fighter and a talented negotiator, a disciplined Jedi who frequently pauses in battle to offer a witty aside. While often impatient with the Senate and its political debates, Obi-Wan firmly believes the Republic must be saved, as it offers the only real chance for the galaxy's citizens to live their lives in peace.

THE OLD TEAM

☆ Few Jedi have seen their names linked as closely as those of Obi-Wan and Anakin. They may sometimes disagree, but in battle they move and fight as one. The demands of the war have mostly separated Obi-Wan and Anakin, but now and again they find themselves fighting back to back once more.

KENOBI'S KIT

Unlike most Jedi, Obi-Wan wears numerous pieces of clone-trooper armor over his robes. He says the armor prevents minor injuries in battle, minimizing distractions.

JEDI CREST

CLONE GAUNTLETS

GENERAL KENOBI

Jedi generals lead the Republic's clone armies. Some generals are overwhelmingly concerned with grand strategies and barely seem to notice the clones they send to fight and die in battle. Not so Obi-Wan Kenobi. He always listens to his clone officers and never risks their lives if he can help it.

FORCE MASTER

☆ As a Padawan, Obi-Wan was often distracted by anxiety. At other times, he was so overeager that he'd find himself in a pitched fight with a shorted-out lightsaber. That was long ago. Now he is famous for his eerie calm in battle, meeting his foes with a raised eyebrow and a cheerful quip—and, of course, with his saber blazing and the Force at his command.

1 Clone troopers duel battle droids in the crystal city, trying to contain the Separatist advance!

2 Skywalker leaps atop the domes of Octuptarra droids, turning a virus droid to silent scrap with each swing of his lightsaber!

"FIRE ON THOSE TANKS!"

Troops led by Obi-Wan and Anakin take Christophsis, but suffer a savage Separatist counterattack.

3 General Loathsom directs his forces, while Anakin and his new Padawan, Ahsoka, are on their first mission together—to disarm the Separatist shield.

4 Can Anakin and Ahsoka find the shield generator protecting the Separatist army before Loathsom's droid legions find them?

THE BATTLE OF TETH

1 The monastery is heavily defended against aerial attack, forcing Anakin's troops to land in the jungle and to attempt a daring tactic: Ascend a half-mile cliff!

2 Two battalions of battle droids defend the monastery. As the clones use ascension cables to scale the cliff, the Separatist machines rain murderous fire down on them!

CLONE TROOPER USING ASCENSION CABLE

RACE TO THE TOP!

Few leaders would try a vertical assault under fire. But between Teth's iron-rich rock outcroppings and the AT-TE's magnetic feet, Anakin sees a way to take the monastery—and dares Ahsoka to beat him to the top.

24

"RACE YOU TO THE TOP."

PADAWAN
SCRAMBLING ATOP
AT-TE

AT-TE EXTERIOR
GUNNER

3 Climbing a vine with Jedi speed, Anakin is glad to see battle droids on STAPs racing to attack him. Now he has a quicker route to the top!

4 Anakin thinks he's beaten Ahsoka to the summit—where a trio of deadly droidekas await. But, fortunately, his Padawan hadn't fallen far behind!

CO-PILOT/GUNNER

PILOT

SHIP'S NAME:
CRUMB BOMBER

LAAT/I

Gunships are officially known as Low-Altitude Assault Transports/infantry, a mouthful few clone troopers bother to remember once they report for duty. A bigger model, the LAAT/c, is designed for carrying cargo such as AT-TE walkers.

VARIABLE-INTENSITY
LASER CANNONS

REPUBLIC GUNSHIPS

EACH OF THESE speedy troop carriers ferries an entire platoon of clone troopers from a Republic cruiser to the battlefield—at top speeds of more than 600 kilometers an hour. They're also tough combat craft, sporting rotating blast cannons, three laser cannons on the chin and tail, and twin missile launchers able to hit targets beyond the horizon.

LUCKY LEKKU

Like all soldiers, clone troopers feel safer when they give their transports names and imagine they have personalities. Nose art is key to a gunship's character, whether the mascot is a Kowakian monkey-lizard dropping bombs or that old soldier favorite, a pretty girl.

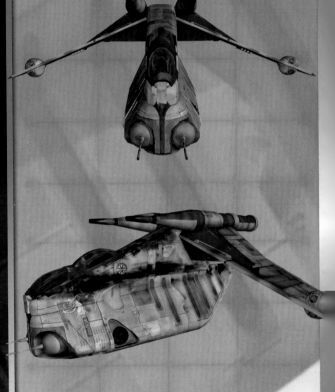

SAFETY MEASURES

✪ Speed and firepower keep gunships safe from most enemies. But they aren't invulnerable—a direct hit can bring one down or blow it to bits. The cockpit capsule can eject as an escape pod, and the side doors are equipped with explosive bolts to blow them clear in the event of a crash-landing.

AT-TE

AT-TE WALKERS ARE imposing six-legged war machines. They protect clone troopers on their way to the front lines and supports them with six laser cannons and a larger missile launcher.

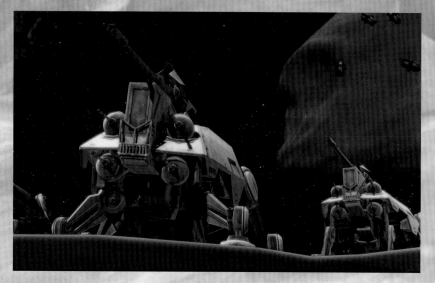

ASTEROID SURPRISE

AT-TEs are meant for ground engagements. But, at Bothawui, Anakin surprises the Separatists by deploying them on ring asteroids, where their magnetic feet allow them to stand firm despite low gravity.

GOING UP!

AT-TEs use their toe magnets, turbo-fired foot grips, and wide stance to climb slopes. However, the techs who designed them never imagined trying them on sheer cliffs, as Anakin orders on Teth.

ALL TERRAIN TACTICAL ENFORCER

★ Rothana Heavy Engineering built the AT-TEs for the Kaminoans who prepared the Republic's clone army. The AT-TE's six-legged stance is inspired by that of the arctic horny whelmer, a hardy beast noted for its footing amid Rothana's icy crags.

AT "

HEAVY PROJECTILE CANNON

PADAWAN RACING HER MASTER TO THE FRONT

TOP PORT FORWARD LASER-CANNON TURRET

WALKER DOWN!

AT-TEs are tough, but they can be destroyed. Weak points include the forward canopy's viewports, needed by the driver when his instruments are jammed, and the ammunition storage hold aft of the front legs.

CLONE CAPTAIN REX

REX IS AN elite clone hardened by campaigns against the Separatists. As Anakin's second-in-command, he has seen the Jedi in action and respects their abilities—though he disapproves of how some of them prefer debating to fighting. Fortunately, his own Jedi general is brave and decisive—sometimes Rex thinks Anakin would make a fine clone.

NEW RECRUITS

Rex leads the famed 501st battalion of clone troopers. He constantly watches for clones who show grit under fire: He is always in need of new men.

THE PROFESSIONAL

Gruff and no-nonsense, Rex combines a commando's gift for improvisation with an infantryman's toughness. Like Anakin, he's fearless, willing to wade into a nest of spider droids or give a top-ranking Jedi his blunt opinion.

LEADING FROM THE FRONT

Many clones are content to follow their Jedi generals' lead—but not Rex. If he had his way, he'd get to the fighting ahead of Anakin. What he couldn't do with Force powers of his own....

ARMY OF ONE

Like any good soldier, Rex knows his weapons. But he also knows gear alone won't keep a clone alive or win a battle. When things go wrong, as they always do, no weapon beats the brain.

JAIG EYES (BATTLE HONORS)

KAMA (FLEXIBLE ANTI-BLAST ARMOR)

CC-7567

The origin of Rex's nickname? Only he knows, and he's not telling.

KAMINO'S FINEST

★ Like many clone officers, Rex's gifts were spotted early by the Kaminoans. Then he was developed through additional training and intensive programmed learning.

CLONE OFFICERS

THE JEDI CAN'T command an entire army of clones by themselves. For help, they turn to both Republic military and specially trained clone officers. These elite clones received advanced training on Kamino. Thanks to enhanced programming, they show more initiative than regular clones. At the suggestion of the Jedi, many have taken nicknames in addition to unit numbers.

ADMIRAL YULAREN

Non-clone Wulff Yularen commands Anakin's fleet—and often worries about the Jedi general's apparent attraction to dangerous tactics. He is a by-the-book officer, increasingly obsessed with security.

COMMANDER WOLFFE

Wolffe is a veteran clone trooper who serves Jedi General Plo Koon on board the *Triumphant*. Wolffe is able in battle and has shown a natural ability for problem solving and strategy.

CLONE COMMANDER CODY

Cody is a scarred veteran of numerous campaigns against the Separatists and Obi-Wan's second-in-command. Officially known as CC-2224, he assumed his nickname after the Kaminoans, who created the Republic's clone army, selected him for special training. Obi-Wan has come to depend on Captain Cody, and has recommended him for promotion.

COMMANDER FOX

Fox desperately wants to return to the front, but he is currently assigned to the Coruscant Guard. He soon finds that Separatist plots reach all the way to the capital.

COMMANDER GREE

Formally known as CC-1004, Gree took his nickname from an ancient alien species, which reflects his interest in alien cultures. He and his 41st Elite Corps normally serve with Yoda.

CLONE TROOPERS

THE IDENTICAL TROOPERS who defend the Republic are thought of by most Core Worlders as little more than living droids, genetically engineered for bravery and loyalty. But their commanders notice that they take names for themselves, bond with their "batchers," and are moved by the same fears and hopes as any young soldier.

AGAINST A METAL STORM

On Christophsis, Obi-Wan witnesses bravery typical of his troops: A charge in the face of wave after wave of droids.

TAKE TO THE SKIES

Clone troopers are trained for a variety of battlefield tactics, from infantry advances and recon scouting to taking enemy positions using personal jetpacks.

JEDI BOND

Many clones develop a strong bond with their Jedi generals, who always lead from the front and have a way of accomplishing things that seem impossible. When Anakin orders his troops to scale a cliff on Teth, the clones are confident that whatever he has in mind will succeed.

POLARIZED
T-VISOR

"SHINIES"

Rookie clones endure the mocking nickname "shinies" until their armor bears the scars of combat.

UTILITY
BELT

CLONE ARMOR

★ Clone body armor is made up of 20 plates of plastoid alloy, fitted over a black body glove pressurized against vacuum. Standard weapons are a DC-15 rifle and blaster pistol.

BATTLE DROIDS

THEY'RE NOT SMART, but they're not supposed to be. Rather, battle droids are simple, sturdy machines designed to overwhelm enemies through sheer numbers. Estimates put the number of droids destroyed in the quintillions. But however many battle droids the Republic destroys, more are always on the way.

COLLATERAL DAMAGE
Grievous has a particular hatred for battle droids, considering them all but useless and often taking out his frustrations on nearby units.

CHEST
PLATE

E-5
BLASTER
RIFLE

B1 BATTLE DROID
★ The first B1 models were built on Geonosis, but droid factories are now found on many Separatist worlds. Some experimental models have tougher armor or special capabilities.

ALAS, POOR 1138

Malfunctioning droids can exhibit odd behavior, from carrying objects to endlessly repeating "Roger roger."

AIM FOR THE JOINTS

A shot to the body is the best way to eliminate a living target, but the chest is actually one of the least-vulnerable parts of a battle droid. Experienced clone troopers prefer to aim for the poorly armored joints between the body and limbs, often leaving their targets literally disarmed.

SUPER BATTLE DROIDS

SUPER BATTLE DROIDS are the heavy hitters of the Separatist infantry. They are also big, dumb, and difficult to destroy. Almost comically aggressive, these thickly armored machines sometimes shove their smaller battle-droid cousins aside in their haste to attack their enemies. Regular battle droids often call them "sir" or "boss," but supers never seem to notice this odd courtesy.

ON THE MARCH

Unlike regular battle droids, supers can operate without a connection to a central control computer. But their tactics are less than brilliant: They often forget about foes who move out of visual range.

POWER OUTAGE

Volleys of laserfire can take out a super battle droid, but their tough armor means such kills are neither quick nor easy. A safer tactic is to disrupt their systems with pulses from EMP grenades, or "droid poppers" in military lingo.

B2 SUPER BATTLE DROID

☆ The B2 was developed after regular battle droids proved no match for capable opponents in combat. Internally, B2s are much the same as their weaker cousins, but are protected by a thick shell of tough acertron armor.

FLEXI-ARMOR MIDSECTION

DUAL LASER CANNON

ASAJJ VENTRESS

ASAJJ VENTRESS HAS been trained in the Force by Dooku, though she's officially neither a Sith nor Dooku's apprentice. Born on a savage world far from the central systems, Asajj hates the Jedi with an animal-like savagery. She has battled Obi-Wan and Anakin before, and dreams of the day she will destroy them.

CURVED LIGHTSABER

DOOKU'S TEST

After Nute Gunray's capture by the Republic, it's Asajj's job to free the Neimoidian. When Dooku's Master, Darth Sidious, doubts her ability to handle the job, Asajj takes to her task with barely controlled fury, eager to earn the Sith title she wants so badly.

BRONZIUM SUN DISC

TWIN SABERS

★ Asajj is a master of Jar'Kai, a combat style that utilizes two paired lightsabers. Her two sabers were a gift from Dooku, and once belonged to another apprentice. The sabers can be joined into a single deadly saberstaff.

RAGE ON RUGOSA

When diplomacy fails, it's always good to have a backup plan, and this one is simple: Dooku tells Asajj to kill the Toydarian king Katuunko rather than see him agree to help Yoda and the Republic. In an instant Asajj's crimson sabers ignite and flash toward the Toydarian's throat.

DAUGHTER OF RATTATAK

Asajj was born on remote Rattatak, where the Republic is only a tall tale told by boastful pilots. A stranded Jedi began Ventress's Force training, but was killed by Rattataki warlords. In taking her revenge, Asajj fell to the dark side.

TOO MANY DROIDS

As ambitious Separatist commanders, Asajj and General Grievous are natural rivals. But they have one thing in common: Both routinely take out their frustrations on unlucky battle droids.

RATTATAKI SASH

IN THE SHADOWS

Anakin and Ahsoka rescue Jabba's son, Rotta, but discover the Huttlet is sick and needs medical care. They work to fit the protesting Huttlet into a clone trooper's backpack for speedier transport—unaware they are being watched.

SPY DROID 4A-7

4A-7 IS A prototype, fresh from Arakyd Industries' droid factories on Mechis III. This droid was made by combining the body and limbs of a Cybot Galactica protocol droid with an oversized head that contains a state-of-the-art cognitive module and equipment designed for surveillance.

THE HUMBLE CARETAKER

4A-7 tells Anakin and his troopers he is nothing but the humble caretaker of Teth's monastery. But something about the bug-eyed droid gives Anakin and Ahsoka the creeps.

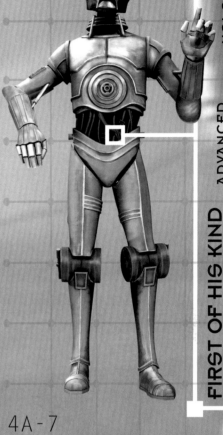

HOLO-RECORDER

ADVANCED SENSOR SUITE

FIRST OF HIS KIND

4A-7's unremarkable exterior hides numerous spy modules.

4A-7

☆ Arakyd specializes in military and explorer droids, but hopes to branch out into espionage. Who better to test a prototype spy droid than the Separatists?

TWILIGHT ENCOUNTER

Padawans should avoid displays of anger, even when insulted by rude mechanicals. But Ahsoka Tano dislikes being mistaken for a servant girl. And tin-plated traitors really make her mad.

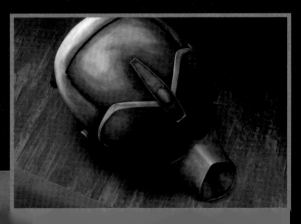

DISHING THE DIRT

4A-7's records Anakin and Ahsoka struggling with the unhappy Rotta, then transmits the recording to Count Dooku on Tatooine. Shown out of context, it looks like the two Jedi are kidnapping a defenseless Huttlet. Jabba is enraged—and 4A-7 has done his dirty work.

COUNT DOOKU

COUNT DOOKU IS the charismatic public face of the Separatists. His speeches have persuaded many planets to abandon the Republic—and his droid armies have brought ruin to many more.

A FALLEN JEDI

The Jedi mourned Dooku as one of the Lost Twenty—Jedi Masters who'd voluntarily left the Order. But they didn't know he had another Master—the mysterious Darth Sidious.

TEMPTING ANAKIN

Few allies are more valuable than fallen Jedi—and few Jedi are mightier than the rash Anakin Skywalker. Dooku sees Anakin's attachments to others as a weakness that might leave him vulnerable to the lures of the dark side.

SON OF SERENNO

Dooku was born on Serenno to wealthy parents who gave him up to the Jedi. After leaving the Order, he reclaimed his noble title and his family wealth, using both to support the Separatist war machine.

CLOAK WOVEN ON VJUN

SIGNATURE CURVED SABER

DOOKU'S SPEEDER

☆ Like his Solar Sailer, Dooku's Flitknot speeder is a product of the factories of Geonosis. These speeders were originally made for patrolling hive territory. Dooku used his bike to escape the Republic's army, and the fallen Jedi has piloted it on many missions since then.

COUNT'S ACES

Dooku is a capable pilot, but his elegant Solar Sailer—a gift from the hives of Geonosis—is made more for cruising the hyperspace lanes than it is for battle. When space combat is called for, Dooku relies on servants such as his MagnaGuards and Vulture Droid starfighters.

RECEIVING VISITORS

Both Obi-Wan Kenobi and Count Dooku promise to rescue Rotta, hoping Jabba's clan will reward their efforts by allowing their starships to use the Hutts' trade routes. Like all Hutts, Jabba demands that visitors flatter him and treat him with the respect he thinks he deserves—such as being called "Mighty Jabba."

ULTRAVIOLET VISION

JAW UNHINGES TO SWALLOW PREY

BROADCAST SPEAKER

POWER AND IMPULSE WIRING

PERILOUS POSITION

☆ Jabba speaks only Huttese to visitors, so a droid is needed to translate his demands. This is a dangerous job: When angry, Jabba often batters translators with a meaty fist or his clublike tail. TC-70 is the latest droid to translate for the Hutt. He won't be the last.

JEDI NANNY

Ahsoka isn't happy to babysit Rotta, but ends up feeling a bit tender toward the helpless Huttlet, despite nicknaming him "Stinky." Rotta needs a doctor—the move from arid Tatooine to cool, wet Teth has made him sick, as has the stress of being kidnapped.

JABBA THE HUTT

JABBA THE HUTT is a powerful crime lord. His Desilijic clan controls trade routes in the Outer Rim. When his son is abducted, Jabba demands help from both the Republic and the Separatists. Whoever rescues Rotta could gain the upper hand in the Clone Wars.

THE HUTTS

These mighty amphibians have controlled a large area of space for thousands of years, and run many of the galaxy's shady businesses. Ruthless and greedy, they have enslaved many other species.

THICK TAIL CAN BE
USED AS CLUB

AGGRESSIVE NEGOTIATIONS

Obi-Wan is known as "the Negotiator," but that nickname doesn't fit the impatient Anakin. Fearing Jabba has killed Ahsoka, Anakin uses the Force to grab his lightsaber away from TC-70 and holds it to Jabba's throat. Dooku, meanwhile, has told Jabba that Anakin has come to kill him. Their misunderstanding could wreck the Republic's hopes for a treaty.

"PEDUNKEE MUFKIN"

Though small enough to fit in a clone trooper's backpack, Rotta the Huttlet is 10 years old, still a toddler in Hutt years. Typically, Hutts spend their first five decades in a parent's brood pouch, emerging from the pouch with a mind equivalent to that of a 10-year-old human. But Jabba wanted his son to experience the galaxy firsthand from birth, a practice virtually unheard of in modern Hutt society.

ANAKIN vs VENTRESS

Ventress, Ahsoka, and Anakin square off after being dropped into a deep pit. When Anakin drops his lightsaber, he looks up to see his enemy's blade descending!

"I've learned much since we last met. Allow me to show you."

Ventress has wanted to fight Anakin again and can barely contain her excitement when she locks blades with him. She dismisses Ahsoka as a pet—but this pet has a lightsaber!

The criminal syndicate that made Teth its home killed their enemies by dropping them into the rancor's pit. Trying to escape with Rotta, Ahsoka opens a giant door. But instead of a way out, she's found the rancor.

SENSITIVE NOSE

JUNGLE RANCOR

MOST RANCORS HAVE dull brown hides, but animal dealers have bred the beasts to produce a number of subspecies: Giants, midgets, horned rancors, and ones with skins in various bright colors.

RAZOR-SHARP SPURS

UNLIKELY DUEL

In the execution pit, Anakin and Ventress greet the rancor's arrival by matter-of-factly leaping onto its broad, bright-striped back and continuing their lightsaber battle. Tired, hungry, and not terribly smart to begin with, the poor confused rancor turns this way and that, following the sound of lightsabers but unable to find who's wielding them.

LOOK OUT BELOW

Fighting is hard enough without having to balance on top of a crazed rancor and dodge battle droids falling from above. The rancor finally flings Ventress and Anakin off its back, but the two have only just began fighting again when Ahsoka jabs her saber into the beast's sensitive snout. It staggers backward and collapses—with a furious Sith apprentice beneath it.

BRIGHT COLOR

Gaudily striped rancors are popular among the crime lords of the Outer Rim, who strive to own the most-exotic beast.

WEBBED HANDS

RANCORS

☆ Rancors are native to the Outer Rim planet of Dathomir, but have spread to many other worlds in the galaxy, often brought by big game hunters, circuses, or zoos. If tamed at an early age, they can bond with other species and be ridden. According to legend, Dathomir's rancors serve as mounts for a strange breed of witches with magical powers.

REPUBLIC FLEET

THE CAPITAL SHIP of the Republic Fleet is the *Venator*-class Star Destroyer, or "Jedi cruiser." Kuat Drive Yards' larger *Imperator* and *Tector*-class Star Destroyers anchor some task forces, but these new ships are still few in number. Until more are deployed, older cruisers, assault shuttles, and fighters fill the gaps.

REPUBLIC CRUISER

These Corellian ships offer a combination of speed and firepower that makes them valuable parts of the fleet. In more peaceful times many were used by Republic diplomats.

DBY-827 TURRETS

The Jedi cruiser's primary line of defense is eight heavy turbolaser turrets, located on either side of the bridge superstructure. The turrets can hit targets over seven light-minutes away.

V-19 PICKETS

The most vulnerable part of a Jedi cruiser is its long dorsal hangar. When a cruiser decants from hyperspace, starfighters immediately scramble to provide a screen around the ship.

WING
HINGE

SECONDARY
LASER
CANNONS

PRIMARY
LASER
CANNONS

BOARDING
RAMP

NU-CLASS ATTACK SHUTTLE

✩ Cygnus Spaceworks designed this heavily armored
attack shuttle, designed for infantry deployments
from space. Clone Captain Rex uses an attack shuttle
dubbed the *Obex*.

V-19 STARFIGHTER

✩ Slayn and Korpil designed
this tough craft for Republic
forces, with the first
prototypes seeing action at
the Battle of Geonosis. It
packs a one-two punch of
cannons and concussion
missiles, with some models
equipped with hyperdrives.

THRUSTER

VENTRAL
AIRFOIL

LASER
CANNON

AIR SUPPORT

The Jedi cruiser's long dorsal hangar deck, marked by a stripe of crimson on the hull, can launch starfighters by the hundreds in short order through the bow doors, with eight heavy turbolasers offering covering fire.

MEDIUM DUAL TURBOLASER

HEAVY TURBOLASER TURRET

JEDI CRUISER

VENATOR-CLASS STAR Destroyers have become the backbone of the Republic Navy, engaging Separatist battleships above countless worlds. They are versatile warships that can launch clouds of starfighters or land for a ground assault. Many Jedi generals have taken *Venators* as their flagships, earning them the nickname "Jedi cruisers."

DUAL BRIDGE

ION CANNON IMPACT

THE FIELD OF BATTLE

The Jedi cruiser's bridge is split into two, reflecting its two missions. The port bridge handles starfighter flight control, while the starboard bridge is the helm. Either offers giant viewports, allowing commanders like Admiral Yularen an ideal vantage point for assessing battles.

VENATOR-CLASS STAR DESTROYER

★ A newcomer to the Clone Wars, the Venator is a product of Kuat Drive Yards. Measuring more than 1,100 meters from bow to stern, it can carry more than 400 starfighters, 40 gunships, and 24 AT-TEs.

DEADLY PATROL

A Vulture Droid can turn its energy torpedoes on ground troops, then take flight to provide air support.

VULTURE FIGHTERS

VULTURE DROIDS ARE ungainly killing machines that serve the Separatists as both air and ground forces. They are able to transform from sleek starfighters into awkward yet deadly patrol craft that walk on scissor-like legs. They are controlled by master signals from a Droid Control Ship. While little match for a Jedi or clone pilot in space, on the ground they are tough foes for clone troopers to tackle.

MAGNETIC IMAGING SENSORS

ENERGY TORPEDO
FIRING CHANNEL

DUEL ON TETH

As Anakin and Ahsoka try to
escape with Rotta, a Vulture
Droid blasts the gunship sent
to retrieve them. It then lands to
duel Master and Padawan.

WALK-MODE
CLAW

DROID STARFIGHTER

☆ Produced by the Xi Char
cathedral factories,
Vulture Droids use
antigravity repulsors to
switch from flight to walk
mode. They can patrol for
more than three hours on
a single charge, though
combat drains their fuel
slugs more quickly.

UPLINK LOST

Vulture Droids are deadly
opponents. They can
operate their weapons
systems so long as they
can receive signals from the
control ship. A foolproof way
to eliminate one? Destroy
the droid brain, located
above the primary sensor
ports in the head.

OBI-WAN: JEDI PILOT

OBI-WAN HATES FLYING—it's either extremely boring or much too exciting. It also requires him to do more tinkering with machines than he would like. Obi-Wan insists that it's far better to simply leave all the hurtling around in space to astromech droids that are built for it.

R4-P17

Obi-Wan's astromech droid, R4-P17, originally sported a conical top typical of R4 models. This top was damaged in an industrial accident and rebuilt by Anakin using a scavenged R2 dome. R4-P17 can often be found patiently beeping and whistling an explanation for astromechs who have wheeled over to inquire about this unusual top.

THE ROAD TO TETH

After negotiating with Jabba the Hutt on Tatooine, Obi-Wan fires up his Jedi starfighter for the short trip across the Outer Rim to Teth, where Anakin and Ahsoka await.

SIDE-SEAT DRIVER

Obi-Wan may be a reluctant pilot, but his former apprentice Anakin Skywalker loves to fly—which would be fine with Obi-Wan if only Anakin weren't always pushing his skills beyond what even he can get away with. Fleeing Grievous's *Malevolence*, the two fall to bickering over everything from Anakin's escape plan to who should man the guns!

HYPERSPACE RING

HYPERSPACE RING

☆ The Delta-7B Aethersprite is too small to have its own hyperdrive, and normally relies on Jedi cruisers for transport through hyperspace. Another option: Docking with a fixed booster ring equipped with its own power plant and supralight engines.

DESTROYER DROID

★ Droidekas were designed by the Colicoids, a species of ruthless insects. The Colicoids adapted their own rolling motion for the droids, which were sold to the Trade Federation and then bought in greater numbers by the Separatists.

PRIMARY SENSOR ANTENNA

BRONZIUM REACTOR HOUSING

QUICK DEPLOYMENT

When moving to intercept enemies, droidekas curl up their heads and legs to become mechanical wheels. They roll with deceptive speed until they reach their target. They then uncurl, activate shields, and open fire.

DROIDEKAS

CLONE TROOPERS REFER to these Separatist units as "destroyer droids" or "rollies." No matter what name is used, it's said with fear: The blasters and energy shields of droidekas usually make even Jedi Knights give way until heavier weapons can be brought to bear.

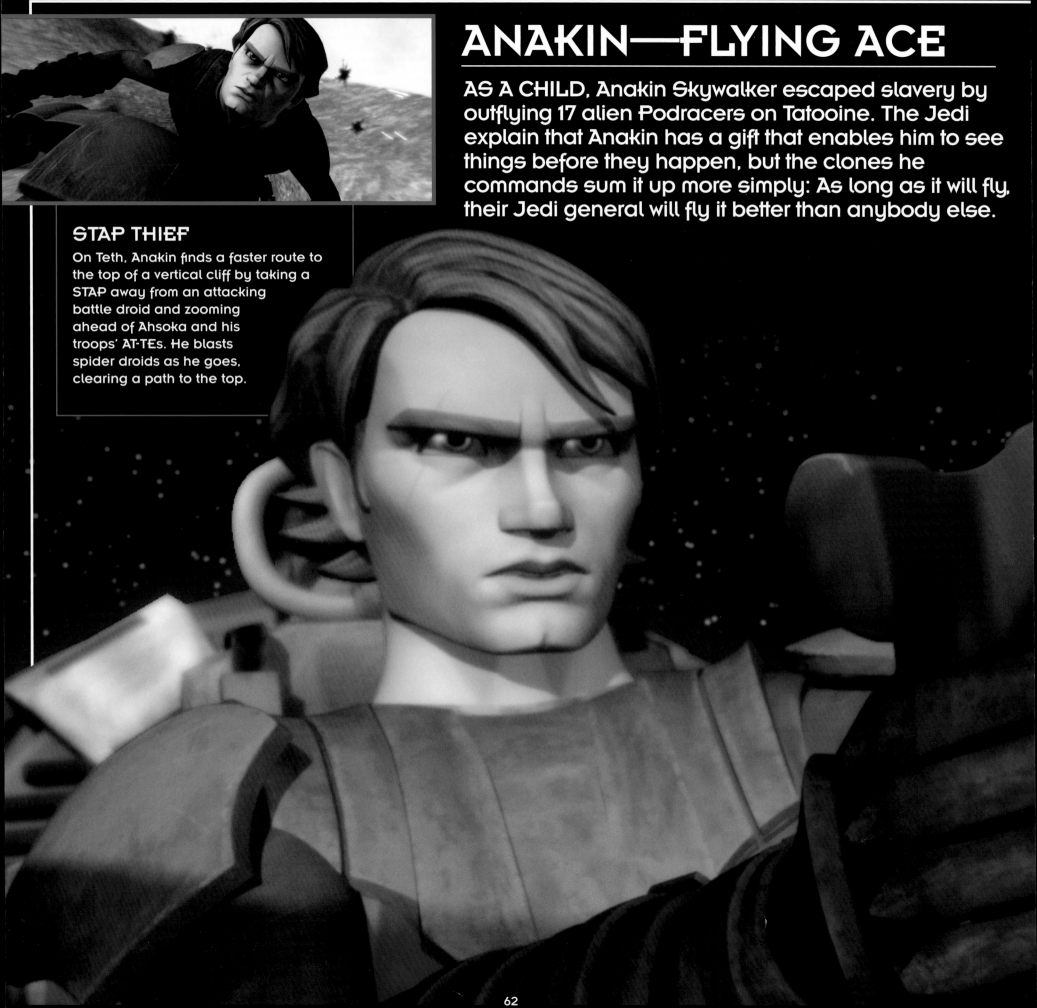

ANAKIN—FLYING ACE

AS A CHILD, Anakin Skywalker escaped slavery by outflying 17 alien Podracers on Tatooine. The Jedi explain that Anakin has a gift that enables him to see things before they happen, but the clones he commands sum it up more simply: As long as it will fly, their Jedi general will fly it better than anybody else.

STAP THIEF

On Teth, Anakin finds a faster route to the top of a vertical cliff by taking a STAP away from an attacking battle droid and zooming ahead of Ahsoka and his troops' AT-TEs. He blasts spider droids as he goes, clearing a path to the top.

CAN-CELL RIDER

Can-cells are native to the soaring forests of Kashyyyk, where the Wookiees consider their appearance a sign of good luck, and have gradually spread to other worlds. They can be trained as mounts, though their light bodies and delicate wings can support larger creatures only for a short time. The can-cells of Teth's jungles are attracted to the buzz of STAPS, mistaking it for their own mating calls. Leaping on a passing can-cell, Anakin reaches out with the Force to convince it to carry him and Ahsoka.

FREIGHTER PILOT

Anakin and Ahsoka escape Teth in the *Twilight*, a dingy freighter that's seen better days. But Anakin comes to like the ungainly old ship, using it in a number of later missions. Ahsoka swears he keeps the *Twilight* around only to prove that yes, he really can fly anything.

ON THE RUN

With old freighters, the question isn't if all the systems are working (they usually aren't), but what systems are most important. Approaching Tatooine, Anakin orders R2-D2 to repair the *Twilight*'s guns first—fixing the rear deflector shields will have to wait for a quieter time.

A LONG WAY DOWN

Fleeing Teth, Anakin discovers the *Twilight* is carrying too much weight for her poorly tuned engines to handle. But as Ahsoka ditches the cargo, one misstep could prove fatal.

THE *TWILIGHT*

ANAKIN FIRST SEES the battered *Twilight* sitting on a landing pad on Teth. Ahsoka wonders if she'll even fly, but the ship is the only way to escape from the planet, and that's what matters. After their escape, Anakin tinkers with the freighter and takes a liking to her—restored to working order and given a few special modifications, she could pack a surprising punch.

PIRATE INSURANCE

A Tal Nami freighter's "swing wing" allows for greater maneuverability and can support an extra blaster cannon as insurance against the threat of space pirates.

HITCHING A RIDE

Searching for R2-D2, Anakin, Ahsoka, Rex, four clone troopers, and R3-S6 pile into the *Twilight* for the voyage to Skytop Station. The old freighter will hold them all comfortably, and attract a lot less notice in Separatist space than a Republic gunship would.

PIVOTING
BLASTER
CANNON

SWING WING
FOLDS UP WHEN
DOCKED

THE *TWILIGHT*

★ The *Twilight* is an old Corellian G9 Rigger freighter and is one of the first ships of its class built with a hyperdrive. It was purchased by Ziro the Hutt to smuggle illegal spice through checkpoints. Its engines were placed outside its main fuselage to allow for more cargo space.

THE JUMP TO HYPERSPACE

WHEN FLEEING TETH in the *Twilight*, Anakin and Ahsoka must escape swarming Vulture Droids and a space battle between Republic and Separatist forces. Unable to land on the *Resolute*, Anakin tells R2 to set a course for Tatooine—and a rendezvous with Jabba the Hutt!

HYPERDRIVE
THROTTLE

NAVI-COMPUTER
DISPLAY

AN INTERSTELLAR SHORTCUT

Hyperspace is another dimension in which real objects cast "mass shadows."
Ships can move through it at great speed but must carefully plot courses—
such as Padmé's to a secret meeting—to avoid colliding with a mass shadow.

SPIDER DROIDS

SPIDER DROIDS ARE the attack dogs of the Separatist armies. These four-legged, two-meter tall mechanicals back up battle droids with cannons that can blast apart light vehicles. Spider droids don't require a central control to function, and are about as smart as a bright domesticated animal. At times they balk when given dangerous tasks.

TRACING ANTENNA

LASER CANNON

INFRARED PHOTORECEPTORS

DSD1-DWARF SPIDER DROID

★ Spider droids were originally used by the Commerce Guild to dig out renegade miners from behind underground barricades, and can see in complete darkness. A larger model offers greater firepower.

DEADLY CLIMB

As Anakin, Ahsoka, and R2-D2 head for the landing platform where the *Twilight* is docked, dwarf spider droids chase after them. The droids' clawed feet allow them to cling to the vertical sides of the landing platform, while their guns fire at the escaping Jedi and their astromech droid.

OCTUPTARRA DROID

These exotic four-legged droids boast laser cannons that can fire in any direction and legs that can cling to overhangs, making them ideal for ambushes. Their most-frightening use, however, is as vessels for biological weapons: They can be equipped with sprayers for pumping out genetically engineered plagues in cities or on the battlefield, which has given rise to their grim nickname "virus droids."

COMBAT TRI-DROID

☆ Tri-droids are frighteningly alien to human observers, but not to the Skakoans of the Techno Union: The droids look like vine-climbers native to methane-shrouded Skako.

OBI-WAN VS VENTRESS

Obi-Wan pursues an old enemy into the castle on Teth after saving Captain Rex and his troopers from battle droids.

"NOW YOU DIE!"

1 Asajj attacks with two blades, but Obi-Wan stands firm against her attack, coolly parrying each crimson blade in turn!

2 On the castle ramparts, Asajj uses the Force to learn of Anakin's escape. Her mission has failed, and now Obi-Wan has her cornered!

TRIDACTYL
HANDS

WISE COUNSEL

Yoda has advised many leaders of the Republic in his long life, and has learned to wait and hear them out before offering advice—often with a crucial insight that no one else has offered.

YODA

YODA IS THE Grand Master of the Jedi Order. He has trained countless Younglings and Padawans. Yoda stands alone in wisdom and experience and is determined to serve the Republic. However, he is troubled by strange ripples in the Force and fears a lasting darkness may await the galaxy and the Jedi who have defended its people for so long.

SMALL
LIGHTSABER

FEELING THE FORCE

Centuries of training have taught Yoda to open himself to the Force, enabling him to accomplish incredible feats. But what he values most is the ability to feel when his fellow Jedi are in trouble, and to sense their location.

ROUGH, SIMPLE
ROBE

SIZE MATTERS NOT

★ Padawans who see Yoda shuffling along with his cane may not believe it, but the little Jedi Master is deadly with a lightsaber. He is able to transform himself into a spinning, leaping blur if combat is required. In battle, he's the equal of anyone in the Jedi Order.

A TROUBLESOME JEDI

Is Anakin Skywalker the Chosen One who will bring balance to the Force? Yoda isn't sure, but he does know young Skywalker is reckless and often lets his emotions run wild. In an effort to teach him control, Yoda decides to give him a Padawan—the young and equally reckless Ahsoka Tano.

THE RELUCTANT GENERAL

To Yoda, violence should always be a last resort. The best outcome of any conflict is to avoid warfare and the suffering it brings. But the ancient Jedi Master knows Count Dooku and the Separatists must be stopped. Now Yoda finds himself as the reluctant leader of Jedi generals such as Anakin Skywalker and Obi-Wan Kenobi and their army of clone troopers.

TEACHER AND TROOPS

On the neutral moon of Rugosa, Yoda accepts a wager from Asajj Ventress: If the Jedi Master beats her troops, the Toydarians will join the Republic; if not, they'll cast their lot with the Separatists. Only three clone troopers accompany Yoda—soldiers he takes as students. From him, they will learn that "size matters not," and that, while they may share the same face, they are unique in their humanity.

CHANCELLOR PALPATINE

PALPATINE WAS ONCE a Senator from Naboo. He was elected Chancellor of the Galactic Republic after the battle of Naboo and now faces the difficult task of leading the Republic against enemies who would destroy it. Palpatine is patient with his critics, insisting that his only desire is to see peace restored to a war-torn galaxy.

ROBES OF OFFICE

THE WAR ROOM

The Chancellor's office on Coruscant is the site of debates between Jedi, military leaders, and Senators about how to win the war.

THE GALAXY'S SERVANT

Palpatine's many duties include working with the Senate to pass laws to fund the war and keep politics from becoming a distraction. He regrets that fighting the Separatists has required him to take up emergency powers, and often speaks of how much he looks forward to the day when he can give up those powers.

LEADING THE JEDI

Palpatine knows that the Jedi are one of the Republic's greatest assets in the war against the Separatists. Because of this, he is careful to be diplomatic when discussing strategy with high-ranking Jedi.

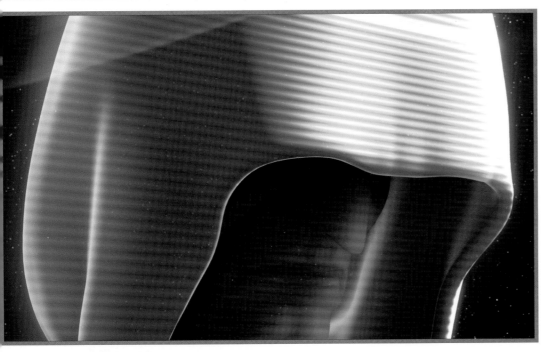

A HIDDEN FACE

Darth Sidious is human. Dooku has met the Sith Lord and knows his identity, but guards the secret closely.

HOLOGRAM SUMMONS

Darth Sidious prefers to speak to servants such as Dooku by hologram. He gives orders for the Separatists' next move and then disappears as quickly as he appeared.

DARTH SIDIOUS

COUNT DOOKU IS the public face of the Separatists and their cause. But a shadowy figure called Darth Sidious works from the darkness, giving orders to Dooku himself. Sidious is a mystery to the Republic. On Geonosis, Dooku told Obi-Wan Kenobi that Sidious was a Sith Lord who controlled the Senate. Most think Dooku was lying and that there is no Sidious. But he is very real.

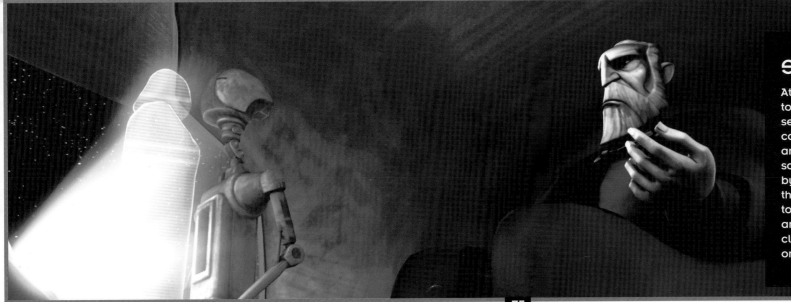

STRANGE TACTICS

At first, Count Dooku dreaded having to tell Darth Sidious about another setback for the Separatists in their campaign to overthrow the Republic and seize Coruscant. But Sidious sometimes seems oddly unconcerned by these losses, telling Dooku that the war is going very much according to his master plan. What is that plan, and how can Jedi victories bring it closer to completion? Dooku can only wonder.

CORUSCANT'S DREGS

Trandoshan slavers, Nikto thugs, sleazy humans, even renegade droids—if galactic lowlifes with fearsome reputations or lots of credits make it to Coruscant, sooner or later they find their way to Ziro's court.

ZIRO THE HUTT

ZIRO IS A tattooed crime lord based on Coruscant. He controls seven key trade worlds belonging to the Desilijic clan between Hutt Space and the Republic capital. He is a Vigo (lieutenant) in the criminal syndicate known as Black Sun. Ziro's endless scheming has made him rich, but his ambitions are so obvious that no one trusts him—least of all his nephew, Jabba.

KRONOS-327

☆ One of Ziro's most-notorious assassins is KRONOS-327, a renegade IG-86 unit. When Kronos fails to eliminate a rival Vigo on Yout 12, Ziro decides the assassin droid is no longer useful so he activates a secret control neutralizing the droid's weapons.

ZIRO'S PALACE

Ziro began his criminal career as a Desilijic loan shark on the Hutt trade world of Sleheyron, where he adopted the tattoos, headdresses, and jewelry of that planet's wealthy Hutts. But he left Sleheyron to pursue his fortune on Coruscant. He purchased a rundown tower that once belonged to the Lantillian Spacers' Brotherhood and remade it as a gaudy pleasure palace.

DOOKU'S PLOT

Ziro agreed to kidnap Jabba's son in exchange for Dooku's promise that the abduction would be blamed on the Jedi and the Huttlet wouldn't survive. Ziro hopes to check Jabba's power within their clan by eliminating his heir.

AN HONORED GUEST

After Palpatine tells Padmé that Jabba has broken off talks with the Republic, she tries to reopen communications by speaking with Ziro. She has no idea Jabba's uncle is plotting with Count Dooku and that she's walking into a trap.

UBRIKKIAN TAIL
SPIRAL RING

SLEHEYRONI TATTOOS

PADMÉ AMIDALA

NABOO ROYAL PISTOL

IN THE SENATE, Padmé is a leading voice for peace. She serves her planet Naboo and champions the cause of the galaxy's least-fortunate citizens. Padmé is opposed to the war, but she knows that, when battle droids are on the march, it's best to leave the talking to her blaster.

TWO GALAXIES?

Padmé fears the galaxy has become two very different places. On Corsucant, Senators vote for new armies before a glamorous night at the opera, while people near the Outer Rim live in terror that war will come to take away everything.

ONCE A QUEEN

☆ The people of Naboo elected Padmé queen when she was just 14 years old—and she helped save the planet from invasion just months after that election. When her term expired, Queen Jamillia asked Padmé to serve Naboo as its Senator.

FAR TOO TRUSTING?

Padmé's best quality is also her biggest weakness. Her ability to see good in people can also blind her to evil intentions. Chancellor Palpatine, for one, has urged Padmé to be more careful, lest she be used by those who claim they want peace.

CORUSCANT PERIL

When talks fail between the Republic and Jabba the Hutt, Padmé rushes to Jabba's uncle Ziro in hopes of ending the crisis, only to be caught in the Hutt's plot.

A LIFE OF SERVICE

Padmé joined Naboo's Apprentice Legislature at the age of eight. While still a young girl, she helped with the Shadda-Bi-Boran refugee crisis. Now, Padmé is determined to bring peace to a troubled galaxy.

SENATORIAL RANK BADGE

AN OLD ADVERSARY

On Rodia, Padmé walks into a trap. Her old family friend, Onaconda Farr, betrays her to Nute Gunray, who still wants revenge for the Trade Federation's long-ago defeat at Naboo. With no Jedi or clone troopers around, Naboo's Senator decides she'll have to rescue herself.

SHAAK-HIDE HOLSTER

PANAKA'S GIFT

When Padmé became Queen of Naboo, she took grueling courses in self-defense and weapons training at the insistence of her captain of the guard, Panaka. Padmé followed Panaka's orders reluctantly, but now thanks him: His training has saved her life many times.

A GALAXY GONE MAD

C-3PO's no battle droid, despite an unfortunate mix-up once at the Battle of Geonosis. So why does he keep finding himself on the front lines of the war with the Separatists? War is cruel and costly—and besides that, it's rude.

OLFACTORY SENSOR

DON'T SHOOT!

After Padmé is ambushed on Rodia, it falls to C-3PO to call for help from Republic forces. He surrenders hastily when challenged by Nute Gunray's battle droids. But after spending years on a harsh desert world with secondhand droid plating (or none at all), C-3PO is reluctant to see his dazzling exterior damaged. Laser blasts do terrible things to a good bronzium finish.

MAIN POWER RECHARGE SOCKET

MADE TO SUFFER

When Jar Jar Binks tries to make friends with Rodia's swamp life, C-3PO gamely prepares to translate, but the reaction is too rude to repeat—indeed, some responses require no translation.

C-3PO

C-3PO IS A golden droid fluent in more than six million forms of communication—and he can worry and fret in all of them. C-3PO was originally programmed for etiquette and protocol. But he serves Padmé Amidala, who has a distressing tendency to get shot at—which makes for far more dangerous situations than simply mixing up a young Wookiee and an adult Tynnan at a diplomatic reception!

WHAT GOES UP...

Stuck to a magnetic hoist as a result of Jar Jar's bumbling, C-3PO can only watch helplessly as battle droids corner the hapless Gungan—and a heavily armored crab droid stalks into the fray. When Jar Jar somehow survives all that, C-3PO calls for help. But he'd better beware—it's a very long drop.

THE ODD COUPLE

Life with Jar Jar isn't easy: If he isn't saying the wrong thing, he's knocking you over in the cockpit of a starship or hitting the wrong button at the worst possible time. But C-3PO knows that the Gungan means no harm and is a devoted friend. Now, if only he'd stop calling him "Three-so."

THE SUM OF HIS PARTS

☆ Some of C-3PO's components bear the ancient stamp of the long-closed factories of Affa—young Anakin Skywalker built him out of parts from junked Cybot Galactica droids. C-3PO's cognitive module may have been stitched together from three scrapped verbobrains, but his fussy personality is all his own.

OH DEAR, OH DEAR

Although C-3PO isn't programmed with combat abilities, he can be useful on a mission—if only to babysit Jar Jar while Padmé gets on with the serious business of planetary negotiations. Though it takes more than a jittery protocol droid to keep Jar Jar out of trouble!

ANAKIN vs DOOKU

1 Count Dooku hopes to steal back Rotta the Huttlet from Anakin, but he's been tricked—Jabba's son is with Ahsoka!

2 Dooku has a backup plan—he aims to win the upper hand by showing Anakin that Ahsoka is fighting for her life.

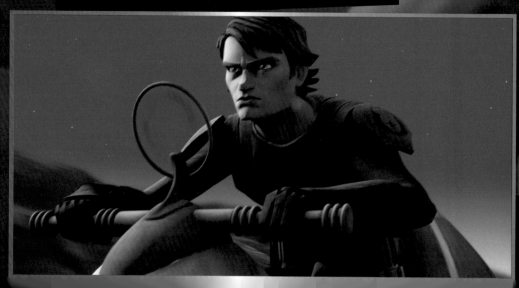

3 Anakin knocks Dooku down and races off to rescue his Padawan. But Dooku only laughs evilly—he has one trap left to spring!

Tatooine's Dune Sea witnesses a clash of lightsabers when Count Dooku intercepts Anakin before the Jedi can reach the palace of Jabba the Hutt.

"SURRENDER THE HUTTLET OR DIE, SKYWALKER."

DARK SIDE POWERS

JEDI WHO SURRENDER to the dark side of the Force command unnatural abilities that make them deadly opponents. Drawing on their own hatred, fear, and passion, they can use the Force to strangle others or dominate their minds. They can also wield the terrible energies of Sith lightning.

DISTRUST YOUR FEELINGS

When dueling him on Tatooine, Count Dooku dips into his Anakin's mind and stirs up his feelings of pain and loss to goad him into an overly aggressive attack—and to tempt the young Jedi into drawing on the dark side himself.

WHERE IS SKYWALKER?

On Teth, Ventress uses the Force to disarm Rex. Then she partially strangles him and orders him to contact Anakin and ask his location. The brave clone captain is a veteran of many battles, but neither his armor nor his training enables him to resist the Force when wielded by a powerful dark side apprentice.

CIRCLE OF DEATH

Both ends of a MagnaGuard's electrostaff blaze with energy that can kill or stun an opponent. MagnaGuards spin these staffs to create a circle of deadly voltage.

MAGNAGUARDS

GENERAL GRIEVOUS TRAVELED with a band of elite bodyguards in his days as a warlord on Kalee. When Grievous joined the Separatists, Dooku ordered a mechanical guard force to be built for the cyborg general. When the new droids proved terrifying in battle, Dooku had more built for his own use.

GANGING UP

MagnaGuards are programmed to fight in groups, with two droids driving an enemy into the electrostaff of a third. Some droids use rocket launchers or blasters instead of staffs.

A KILLING BLOW

MagnaGuards can keep fighting even without their heads—they have a back-up eye set in their chests. On Tatooine, Ahsoka avoids this problem by cutting one in half.

TAKING FLIGHT

While designed mainly for hand-to-hand combat, MagnaGuards can be programmed to pilot vehicles or starfighters. Count Dooku has put his MagnaGuard squads to work as fighter pilots. The Separatist leader has found the droids' combat instincts make them highly effective in space battles.

IG-100

✮ Holowan Mechanicals developed the MagnaGuard using systems from the earlier IG Lancer Droids. But these new droids have stronger armor, better programming, and the ability to learn from combat experience. Even veteran clone troopers fear them.

JEDI'S BANE

MagnaGuards are tough opponents even for a Jedi Knight wielding a lightsaber. The two deadly ends of an electrostaff make parrying with a laser sword difficult, because the energy tendrils deflect saber blades. Even the staff itself is made of durable phrik alloy, which can withstand several cuts from a lightsaber before being severed.

DOWNFALL OF ZIRO THE HUTT

"IT WAS COUNT DOOKU!"

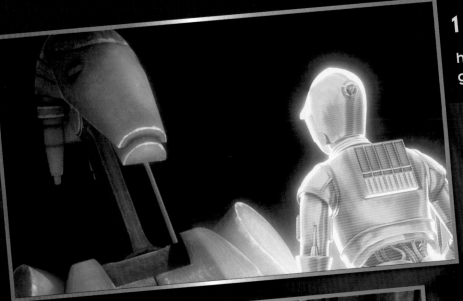

1 Captured by Ziro, Padmé tricks the Hutt's battle droids into activating her holoprojector—then yells for C-3PO to get help.

2 Angered by Padmé's trickery, Ziro decides she's too dangerous to be left alive. Would he dare kill a Senator? You bet he would.

3 Suddenly, explosions! C-3PO arrives with a squad of clone troopers, who free Padmé and foil Ziro's plot.

Ziro thought that plotting with Count Dooku might enable him to destroy Jabba. But a prisoner's quick thinking leaves him to face Republic justice.

A JEDI BOND

YODA WORRIES ABOUT Anakin's emotional attachments to everyone from Padmé and Obi-Wan to R2-D2. So he decides Anakin should take a Padawan. Yoda's hope is that, by letting go of Ahsoka when she becomes a Jedi Knight, Anakin will learn to let go of other, more-dangerous attachments as well.

WINNING RESPECT

Once Anakin gets over his annoyance at having to take an apprentice, he comes to appreciate Ahsoka's bravery and spirit. But the brash young Padawan must prove herself by her actions to win the respect of others, such as Captain Rex and higher-ranking members of the Jedi Order.

HOW TO DISOBEY

Ahsoka is one of the few Jedi who might be as headstrong as Anakin. This is no accident: The Jedi hope that in teaching Ahsoka obedience to the Council's orders, Anakin will reconsider his own disobedience. Instead, Anakin teaches Ahsoka that there are ways to disobey without being obvious about it.

A JEDI'S SECRETS

Returning to Tatooine clearly bothers Anakin, but he refuses to discuss his feelings with Ahsoka. Even Jedi bonds have their limits.

WAR ROOM

ALL COMMANDERS NEED a war room where they can study the battlefield and plan strategy. Hologram technology allows a three-dimensional view of battles as they happen. In the *Resolute's* war room, Anakin, Ahsoka, and Rex are joined remotely by Obi-Wan to discuss the fighting raging below them on Bothawui.

PLAN OF ACTION

While it's useful to be able to watch a battle from the war room, commanders sometimes disagree about what course of action should be taken. At the Battle of Bothawui, Anakin believes his battle-weary troops must fight on to keep the Separatists from taking an entire sector. But Obi-Wan advises retreat.

THE HOLONET

☆ The technology that allows commanders to meet by hologram is a faster, more-robust version of the HoloNet, which allows people to speak in real-time despite being millions of light-years apart. The HoloNet is one of the Republic's greatest achievements.

CLONE TROOPERS IN RECON POSITION

TRACKING POSITIONS

The confusion of war can make it difficult to tell if an overall strategy is working. So soldiers in the field rely on officers in war rooms to give them a sky-eye view of the battle they're waging.

AN OUTSIDE VIEW

When commanders can't be present, they can join the discussion as holograms. This allows them to see the holo-map of the battlefield and to interact with their fellow commanders.

AT-TE WALKER

CLONE TROOPER

THE BATTLE BELOW

The troops on Bothawui are tired and outnumbered. With a Separatist fleet on its way, Anakin argues for a bold course of action.

SEPARATIST BATTLESHIPS

DOOKU'S FLEET IS drawn from the systems and companies that support the Separatists. The backbone of the fleet is the Banking Clan's frigates: Warships that once guarded Clan vaults and threatened worlds with substantial debts.

DROID DUTY

Separatist warships are operated by what the Republic would call skeleton crews—central computers and droids do most of the work.

COMMAND BRIDGE

PROW TURBOLASERS

DEADLY CARGO

Banking Clan Frigates can carry as many as 150,000 armed battle droids. When they are in transit, these soldier droids remain in a deactivated state until they receive the signal to deploy. The battle droids are packed into Multi-Troop Transports and tanks, which are carried to the surfaces of doomed planets by hulking double-winged C-9979 landing ships.

MALEVOLENCE

✩ Quarren Separatists built the *Malevolence* on Pammant, but it isn't their only creation—or Grievous's only flagship. The general has also assaulted the Republic from a pair of converted carriers: *Invisible Hand* and *Lucid Voice*.

PORT ION CANNON

KILLING MACHINE

Grievous's tough armor, lightning-fast reflexes, and combat training make him a match for even a Jedi Master.

GENERAL GRIEVOUS

GRIEVOUS IS THE savage commander of the Separatist military and he looms as a figure of terror in the Republic. The cyborg general hates Jedi, taking his kills' lightsabers as grim trophies.

MAGNETIZED TALONS

REINFORCED KNEE PLATING

GRIEVOUS'S FIGHTER

Grievous's ace in the hole is a battle-scarred Belbullab-22 starfighter. However, Grievous isn't an ace pilot. He uses the ship mainly as a means of escaping from doomed battles.

ARMS
CAN
SPLIT
IN TWO

SEPARATIST GENERAL

☆ Grievous hates droids, even though he commands them. (He makes a rare exception for his MagnaGuards.) Grievous made the choice to be rebuilt as a cyborg, but reacts with savage fury if mistaken for a droid himself.

STEEL WARLORD

Grievous was once an organic being, earning his reputation as a warlord in the planet Kalee's brutal war against its Huk neighbors. After nearly being killed in a shuttle crash, he was rebuilt by Geonosian engineers and agreed to serve the Separatists in exchange for aid for the Kaleesh. While not Force-sensitive, he is formidable with a lightsaber, as Ahsoka discovers on Skytop Station.

BATTLE OF BOTHAWUI

1 Grievous's ships move through Bothawui's rings, trusting their forward shields for protection.

2 At Anakin's signal, AT-TE walkers hidden on the ring asteroids open fire on the Separatists' unprotected sterns. Grievous has been outflanked!

3 Chasing after the retreating Grievous, Anakin's starfighter is battered by debris from an exploding frigate and breaks up—with Anakin and R2 still aboard!

Determined to hold Bothawui against Grievous, Anakin has a plan to catch the Separatist fleet in a crossfire. But what price must he pay for victory?

A MISSING DROID

Obi-Wan lectures Anakin for being upset about losing R2, reminding him that Jedi avoid attachment. But he's alarmed to learn that R2 never had a memory wipe and contains top-secret military information.

R3-S6

AFTER R2-D2 IS lost on a mission at Bothawui, the Republic sends Anakin a new astromech droid: R3-S6. Most R3 units have clear, transparent domes, but with astromechs needed for the war effort, units with minor defects are sent to the front as soon as possible. So "Goldie" arrives with a scavenged R2 dome.

R3'S SECRET

R3 is actually a spy: Separatist agents in the Republic military sabotaged his programming and arranged for him to be sent to Bothawui.

RGB
PHOTORECEPTOR

STATUS
DISPLAY

LOUD-
SPEAKER

EXTENDIBLE
THIRD LEG

MANY MISTAKES

R3 seems like he's trying his best, but keeps making dangerous errors. Aboard the *Vulture's Claw*, he turns on the overhead lights while accessing the computer system. Harmless enough—but next he wakes up two IG-86 assassin droids.

GHA NACHKT

☆ Gha is a Trandoshan scavenger who hunts through fields of debris left after space battles, searching for something he can sell. Anakin, Ahsoka, and R3 encounter him and his battered freighter *Vulture's Claw* while searching for R2-D2 in the Bothawui system.

CALL HIM "GOLDIE"

Ahsoka tries to get Anakin to warm to R3, whom she nicknames "Goldie" for his colors and his role in Gold Squadron. She notes that R3 units' cognitive modules are faster and more powerful than the old R2 units.

ALL-TERRAIN MAIN DRIVE TREAD

DROID DUEL!

After R2-D2 is rescued from the Separatists on Skytop Station, he encounters his replacement—by now revealed as a traitor—on an exterior platform. The two droids square off in a furious duel, using everything in their mechanical arsenals from gripper arms, magnetic grapples, and oil sprayers to electric prods, drills, and saws.

GHA NACHKT

TRANDOSHAN SCAVENGER GHA Nachkt hunts through debris fields left behind after space battles. He searches for parts of ships and droids he can salvage and sell to the highest bidder.

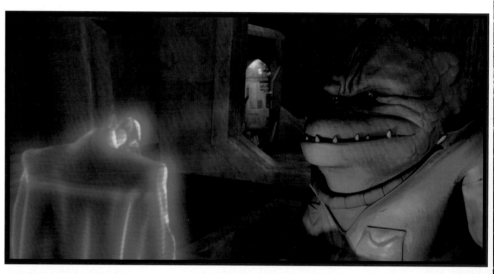

NOT THE DROID WE'RE LOOKING FOR

Anakin and Ahsoka find Nachkt's ship plundering the debris after the space battle of Bothawui. They hunt for R2-D2 in his junk-filled hold. Finding nothing, Anakin threatens Nachkt—to no avail.

STASHED AWAY

In Nachkt's secret storage, R2 is hidden away and locked down with a restraining bolt. Nachkt contacts Grievous to tell him that he's en route to their rendezvous point with very interesting salvage—an astromech wanted by an upset Jedi.

READING MINDS

On Skytop Station, Nachkt pokes through R2's memory. What he finds astonishes him—Republic military secrets worth an enormous amount to the Separatists.

A DISCERNING EYE

Nachkt likes to call himself "a purveyor of previously owned collector's items." He thinks this sounds better than "battlefield scavenger," "junk ghoul," or other nasty names he's heard.

EXTREMELY STAINED COVERALLS

TOOL BELT

VULTURE'S CLAW

☆ Nachkt's battered freighter, *Vulture's Claw*, is so old and has been through so many refits that identifying its original maker is little more than guesswork now. Its dingy holds bulge with years' worth of battlefield debris for customers to pick through.

SOMETHING EXTRA

Anakin has always refused to erase R2's memory. His choice could now change the course of the war, as vital Republic secrets are in Grievous's hands. Nachkt has made the biggest find of his career and thinks he's earned a little extra. General Grievous seems to agree....

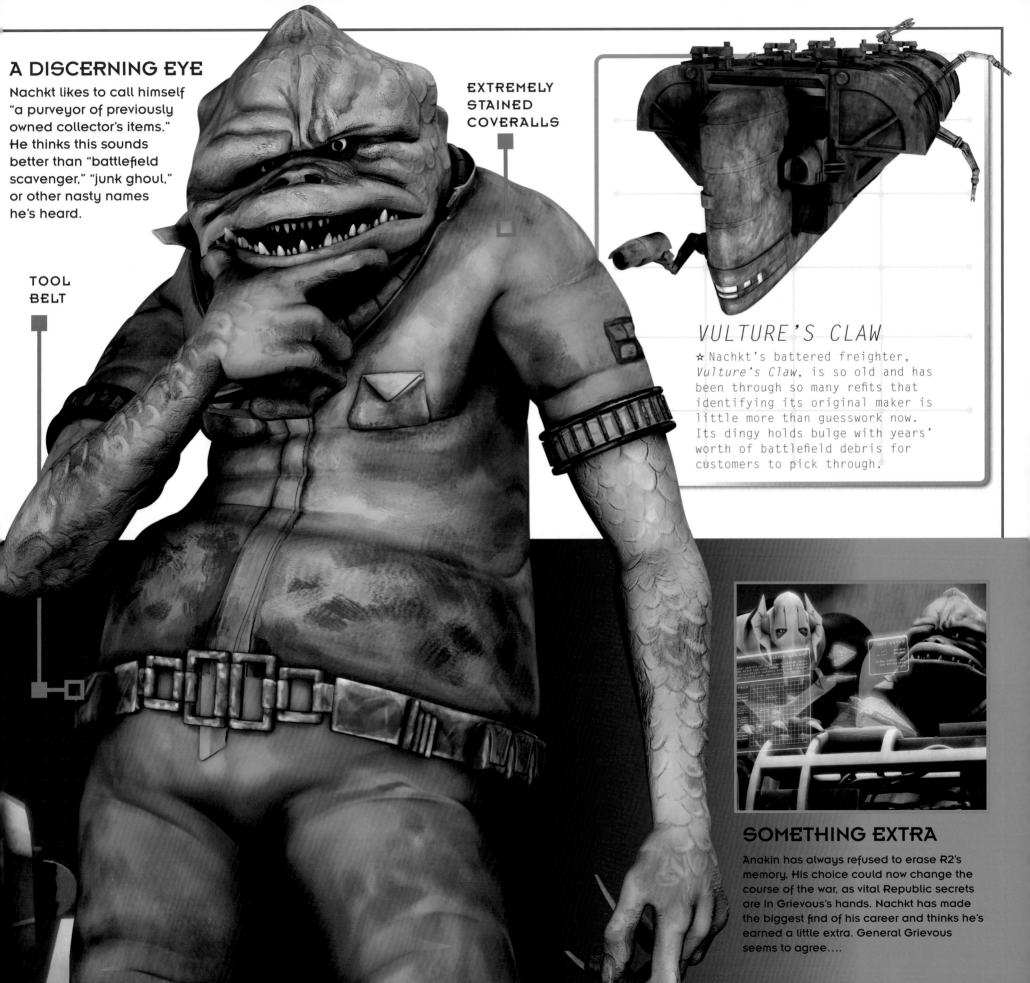

VULTURE FIGHTERS IN FLIGHT MODE

IN SPACE, VULTURE Droids seem graceful—but few stop to admire that grace, for fear of being blasted by laser fire. Separatist warships launch these deadly drone fighters in huge waves against any who dare offer opposition.

SHORT-RANGE FIGHTERS

☆ The Xi Char factories designed Vulture Droids to fly for just 35 minutes between recharges. To fuel up, they nestle upside-down beneath power grids on their home starships, occasionally testing their wings and other systems like ghastly, half-asleep bats.

FLIGHT MODE CLAW

DISTANCE LEARNING

In flight, Vulture Droids take orders from a Droid Control Ship computer using a dull but effective plan. The first droid waves use only basic attack and defense programs. The computer then tweaks strategies based on those attacks, launching a deadlier assault.

BOARDING CRAFT

A Colicoid creation (like the droideka), this Separatist boarding craft looks like a flying spike—until that spike divides into four sharp prongs that can stab through an enemy hull, revealing a central hatch used by a boarding party. The craft is a mechanical version of the toothspike raptor, a predatory insect that lurks beneath the sands of Colla IV's deserts—a nightmare vision transplanted into outer space.

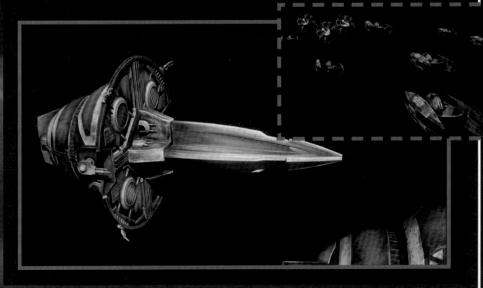

COME ON, THREE-SO!

Jar Jar likes C-3PO, despite his fussy ways: He helps Jar Jar talk to strange creatures, and the golden droid quickly gets over it when there's one of those accidents that happen around Jar Jar.

SERVING NABOO

★ Padmé has faith that others will see Jar Jar's kindness and decency, but she still takes it on herself to keep her old friend out of trouble. Jar Jar can be rashly brave when he'd be better off thinking things over; and some situations call for her diplomacy, not his enthusiasm.

MACKINEEKS!

Rodia seems like a nice enough planet—who doesn't like moist air and warm seas? Except the place is crawling with battle droids, and Jar Jar remembers all too well how much trouble they caused on his homeworld, and how much their masters hate his friend Padmé. Jar Jar knows he has to do something to save the day. But what should he do?

MEESA SORRY!

Oh, those lettal bitty axadentes. They got him banished from his home in Otoh Gunga, and now they seem to keep happening wherever he goes in the galaxy. Jar Jar isn't sure it's really all his fault. Take this hangar on Rodia—why leave giant magnets where they could fall on a ship? Dissa nutsen!

JAR JAR BINKS

JAR JAR IS a Gungan representative from Naboo, and has long been a friend of Padmé's. Even Jar Jar's pals admit he's silly, often simple, and should never be allowed near machinery— but they love him for his kind heart and loyalty.

HAILLU

CEREMONIAL NABOO SCARF

UNDER THE SEA

Gungans love the water, and no one who saw Jar Jar in his natural element would call him clumsy. Rodia's lagoons remind Jar Jar of Naboo, down to the bad boogie monsters who live in the depths. And what's with these droids dropping things like thermal detonators? They say Jar Jar's accident-prone!

MASTER BOMBAD

The Jedi robe someone left on Padmé's ship seems like a great way for Jar Jar to disguise himself while going to rescue his old friend. Sure, having an actual Jedi around would be better, but Jar Jar will have to do his best.

GUNGANS

Above all else, Gungans are flexible. They breathe both air and water, they eat both water plants and shellfish, they speak their own language and pidgin Basic, and they're comfortable on land and under the sea. Their bodies are flexible, too—Gungan skeletons are made of cartilage, allowing them to twist in ways that can leave other species doing double-takes.

ONACONDA FARR

ONACONDA FARR IS a Senator from the Outer Rim planet of Rodia. He has been one of Padmé's family friends since she was a little girl. But when war comes to Rodia, Onaconda must find a way to save his starving people—even if it costs him his honor.

RODIANS

☆ Rodians evolved from reptilian ancestors, and are famous for their skill as hunters. Rodian society is based around clans.

SILOOD

Onaconda's longtime attendant, Silood is always at the Senator's side and has become his confidant.

RELUCTANT BETRAYAL

With the Republic unwilling or unable to help Rodia's people, Farr turns to the Trade Federation's Nute Gunray for aid. The Neimoidian promises immediate shipments of food and medical supplies, but only if Padmé is delivered as a prisoner of war.

SORRY, MY SWEET

Betraying Padmé hurts Farr badly. But the Rodian is confident that he can use his status as a Senator to make sure no harm comes to Padmé while she is held captive by the Separatists.

CAUGHT IN THE MIDDLE

Rodia sits just across the border of the Outer Rim, right between the forces of the Republic and those of the Separatists. Caught in the middle, the marshy planet is left starving, and is desperate for help from any source.

NUTE GUNRAY

VICEROY NUTE GUNRAY pushed the Trade Federation into conflict with the Republic years ago, a dispute that led to the Separatist movement and the Clone Wars. The cause has been costly for Gunray: He's been harassed by Republic courts and seen profits decline. Privately, he regrets becoming Darth Sidious's pawn, but the Trade Federation has made its choice and can now only hope for the best.

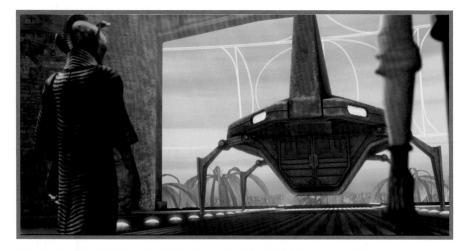

TRADE FEDERATION LANDING SHIP

Neimoidian landing craft mimic the look of giant domesticated beetles native to Neimoidia and its colony worlds. The ships are piloted by instruments from a sealed-off cockpit.

NEIMOIDIANS

Neimoidians are trained for ruthlessness from birth. Grubs live together in communal hives for their first seven years. Those who fail to secure food are allowed to die. Adults stockpile possessions and are always searching for more. Neimoidians never apologize for their greed. After all, they owe their lives to it.

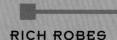

RICH ROBES

OBSESSION

Gunray's obsession is to avenge his humiliation at Naboo and in the courts by arranging the death of Padmé Amidala. To a Neimodian, revenge should never get in the way of profits—and by that measure, Gunray's obsession long ago crossed the line and became foolishness.

OLFACTORY
GLANDS

NEIMOIDIAN
HEADDRESS

BETRAYAL

Caught between Republic and Separatist forces, the planet Rodia faces starvation. Seeing a chance for revenge on an old enemy, Gunray approaches Onaconda Farr with a proposition: Deliver Padmé, and the Trade Federation will help the Rodian people. Desperate to bring aid to his planet, Farr agrees. But sometimes the honorable thing is to go back on a bargain one shouldn't have made in the first place.

STOP THAT JEDI!

Most Neimoidians fear the Jedi, viewing their monastic lives and refusal to seek power as borderline-insane. Gunray has hated them ever since his Naboo plot was wrecked by a child—a boy who's now a Jedi Knight.

"Jedi!!
Where'sa Jedi?
Meesa not a Jedi!"

1 Padmé is betrayed by Onaconda Farr and is chained in a detention cell despite Farr's protests!

2 Padmé escapes, using a lockpick and playing on droids' anxiety about a Gungan "Jedi" on the loose.

3 As Gunray's battle droids hunt Jar Jar, Padmé turns the tables and begins hunting them!

INTRIGUE ON RODIA

Padmé knows she can only hold her own in a firefight for so long. What she needs is reinforcements—and she won't be picky about where they come from.

KWAZEL MAW

KWAZEL MAWS ARE feared predators of the Rodian seas. They are usually found in the depths, where their great eyes locate prey that they stun with flashes of their bioluminescent markings. Kwazel Maws sometimes wander into the planet's lagoons, where heat from power generators often proves to their liking.

RODIAN PREDATOR

✫ Kwazel Maws can live 100 years and grow to more than 85 meters in the deepest seas of Rodia. These clumsy swimmers generally cling to undersea canyon walls with their prolegs until their sensitive antennae detect movement nearby.

BIOLUMINESCENT MARKINGS

1 Jar Jar seeks refuge from Nute Gunray's battle droids in the lagoon under Senator Farr's compound. There, he barely escapes a hungry Kwazel Maw—whose mood turns to fury when thermal detonators send damaging shock waves through the water.

2 Collapsing pillars bury the luckless lagoon monster, but a Kwazel Maw isn't easy to kill. As Jar Jar watches, the great beast shakes off the debris and shoots toward the surface.

3 On the surface, the Kwazel Maw eats tiny, hard-shelled creatures whose stings only make it angrier. As it spits out the bad-tasting shellfish, Jar Jar clings to its antennae for dear life.

Jar Jar's rescue mission hasn't gone particularly well—but sometimes sea monsters can come in handy.

"Hold it right there, Viceroy."

Nute Gunray hoped to witness Padmé's execution on Geonosis. Now, he wishes he'd never sprung this particular trap.

1 This time, Gunray will make sure Padmé perishes. He orders his mechanical minions to carry out the death sentence. They take aim…

2 …but are interrupted by a mysterious hooded Jedi! The "Jedi" raises his arms, causing the very stones of the courtyard to shake and rumble!

3 Gunray watches in horror as the monster summoned by the "Jedi" destroys his droids and his shuttle. Before he can run, he's looking down the barrel of Padmé's blaster!

TANK BATTLE ON RUGOSA

"Size is not everything, mmm?"

1 Ventress suggests a bet: If Yoda escapes her best troops, Toydaria will aid the Republic. If the droids prevail, Katuunko will join Dooku!

With the loyalty of King Katuunko hanging in the balance, Yoda battles hordes of Separatist droids sent to destroy him.

2 In Rugosa's reef canyon, it's one small Jedi against three tanks. Are those tanks ever in trouble!

3 Yoda leaves Asajj's trio of tanks in flames and King Katuunko chuckling. But Ventress isn't beaten yet: Time to send in the destroyer droids!

IN THE LAIR OF GRIEVOUS

1 In the gloomy maze underneath his castle, Grievous faces the two Jedi and a trio of clones. Grievous raises his sabers, but Kit has other ideas!

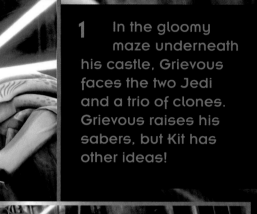

2 The clones fire their ascension cables, trussing up Grievous. Then they try to subdue the cyborg general like a wild animal!

In a remote corner of the Outer Rim, Jedi Kit Fisto and Nahdar Vebb are drawn into Grievous's trap: To fight his pet roggwart named "Gor."

3 With his companions gone, Kit decides it's best to fight another day. But Grievous awaits him in the Vassek fog!

4 Calling in his MagnaGuards, Grievous has Kit cornered. Will the monstrous cyborg add a new saber to his hoard?

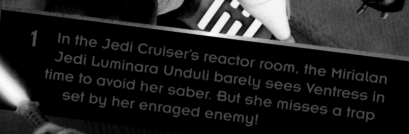

1 In the Jedi Cruiser's reactor room, the Mirialan Jedi Luminara Unduli barely sees Ventress in time to avoid her saber. But she misses a trap set by her enraged enemy!

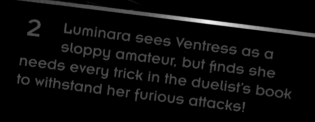

2 Luminara sees Ventress as a sloppy amateur, but finds she needs every trick in the duelist's book to withstand her furious attacks!

"NOW YOU FALL!"

Ventress boards the ship carrying Nute Gunray to Coruscant for trial. Her orders are to free him—or silence him.

3 Vision clouded by a blast of steam, Luminara realizes her enemy is the stronger fighter. That could prove a lesson learned too late for the Jedi!

LIGHTSABERS

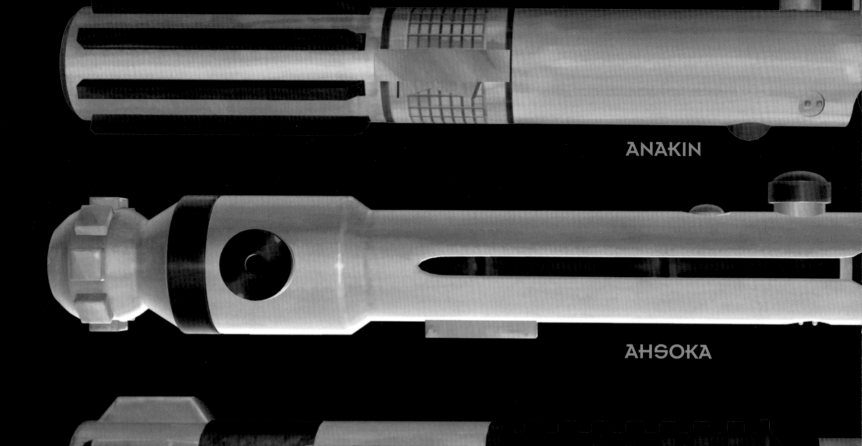

ANAKIN

AHSOKA

OBI-WAN

LIGHTSABERS ARE THE elegant weapons of the Jedi—and their deadly enemies, the Sith. They have a blade of pure energy focused by a special crystal that gives them their color and their ability to cut through almost anything.

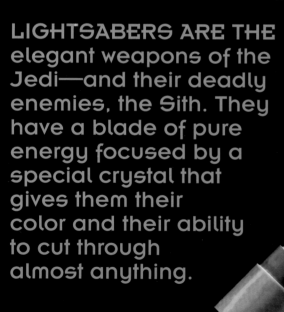

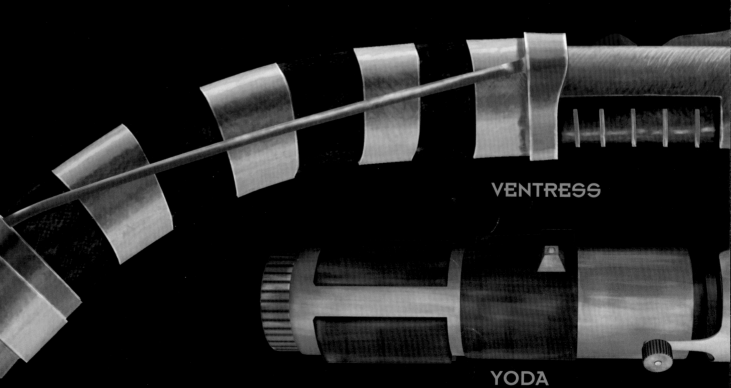

VENTRESS

YODA

SUPERWEAPONS

THE *MALEVOLENCE*'S ION cannon throws the Republic's military strategies into chaos. So long as the giant warship is loose somewhere in space, no Republic fleet is safe. For centuries, superweapons have held a promise for those willing to spend billions of credits: To change the course of a war with a weapon that your enemy can't defend against.

ION CANNONS

☆ Ion cannons have been part of interstellar warfare for centuries. But a ship-mounted cannon with such immense power and so short a recharge time is a new factor in battle. It leaves Republic strategists scrambling to study the technology.

A WEAKNESS?

Running the gigantic power plant required for a weapon like the *Malevolence*'s ion cannon is a delicate task—which leads Anakin to hope that destroying part of the system could wreck the weapon.

AT-TE

PLO KOON

PLO KOON IS a Kel Dor from Dorin and a member of the Jedi Council. He is known equally for his skill with a lightsaber and a starfighter's cannons. Having seen friends such as Qui-Gon Jinn and Micah Giiett die in Separatist plots, he believes Dooku's treason must be met with the full might of the Republic military and the Jedi Knights.

THICK KEL DOR HIDE

SCAVENGED FOREARM ARMOR

I AM THE LAW

A Jedi with a rigid sense of right and wrong, Plo believes decisive action is the best course in a galaxy at war.

BREATH OF LIFE

Dorin is a chilly world in the galaxy's Expansion Region. Its air is thin, so Plo wears goggles and an antiox mask for protection against the oxygen-rich atmospheres of most inhabited planets. But his thick skin gives him some advantages: He can survive in the vacuum of space far longer than an unprotected human.

HEAT-RESISTANT JEDI ROBES

HUNT THE HUNTERS

After the *Triumphant* is destroyed by Grievous's battleship, Plo, Commander Wolffe, and two troopers flee in an escape pod and tumble through the Abregado system, hunted by battle droids. Rather than wait for death, Plo decides they'll meet it, making a desperate stand silhouetted against the stars.

THE BLADE OF DORIN

Plo is one of the Jedi's best pilots. He prefers the cockpit of his starfighter to the deliberations of the Council chamber. Few sights frighten Separatists more than Plo's daggerlike fighter, trailed by his handpicked squadron of clone pilots. Plo knows the galaxy's trade routes well: He warns Anakin and Shadow Squadron that the Balmorra Run cuts through the nesting grounds of the Nebray mantas, sparing all a potentially fatal surprise.

PLO'S STARFIGHTER

★ Many Jedi have raved about the Eta-2 Interceptors beginning to roll off the assembly lines at Kuat Drive Yards, but Plo swears by his Delta-7B Aethersprite. Another of Plo's quirks is his refusal to memory-wipe R7-F5—a fellow veteran of numerous battles.

KOH-TO-YA

While grateful for Anakin and Ahsoka's help at Abregado, Plo worries that Anakin's plan to attack the *Malevolence* is too aggressive, warning that even minimal casualties might leave too few ships to engage the battleship. Many in the Republic consider clones expendable, but Plo will not sacrifice them so cheaply.

ESCAPE FROM *TRIUMPHANT*

1 Plo Koon and his men can only watch as the Jedi Cruiser *Triumphant* vanishes in a ball of fire just seconds after their evacuation.

2 Their escape pod tumbles through the debris field, as they hunt for a sign that others have survived their encounter with the *Malevolence*.

3 As Plo watches in horror, battle droids cut through the windows of another pod, dooming those inside to a grim death in space.

Plo Koon and three troopers flee their ruined cruiser, only to find themselves hunted by battle droids—with orders to leave no survivors!

1 Anakin and Ahsoka hunt for survivors, but a Separatist boarding ship finds the pod first. Cornered, Plo and two clones fight the droids in space!

At Abregado, Plo Koon's task force is destroyed by Grievous's flagship. The Jedi and his troops are left adrift in an escape pod, hunted by battle droids.

HUNTER AND HUNTED

2 Plo uses the Force to push a trooper into space, where he opens fire on the droids!

3 With the droids destroyed, Plo cuts the pod free of the boarding ship. But air is running out—will Anakin and Ahsoka find them in time?

NEBRAY MANTAS

THE REPUBLIC DISPATCHES a strike force led by Anakin to destroy the *Malevolence*. Hoping to cut off Grievous before he assaults a key medical station, Anakin leads a flight of Y-wing bombers through the Kaliida Nebula, using a smuggler's shortcut he heard about years ago on Tatooine. But those pilots left out an important fact: The nebula is the nesting ground of the Nebray mantas!

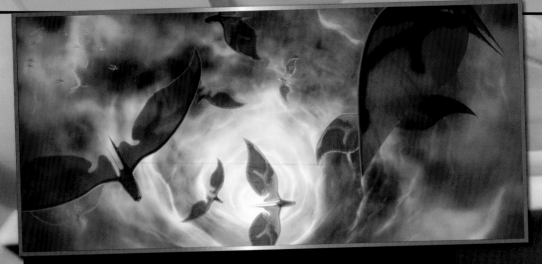

1   Racing through the nebula's heart, Anakin's pilots are startled to find giant mantas swarming around their bombers!

BOMBS AWAY!

Determined to stop Grievous, the Republic outfits Anakin with a squadron of new Y-wings, fighters designed to pound their targets with a barrage of bombs. Even R2-D2 is impressed by the vessels, but an annoyed Ahsoka learns she won't get to fly one—instead, she'll be Anakin's gunner.

2 The big gas-gulpers mean no harm, but tell that to a clone pilot who's just suffered a near-fatal collision with one!

3 Shadow Squadron emerges from the nebula down several ships and rattled from their close encounter with the mantas. And Grievous still awaits!

Y-WING ATTACK

Grievous's flagship *Malevolence* has become the terror of the Outer Rim. When Grievous threatens a key medical station, Anakin decides to attack the giant ship with a flight of Y-wing bombers.

1 As the bombers approach, Grievous fires his flagship's ion cannon, destroying two Y-wings and several of his own droid starfighters. The Y-wing pilots zero in on the *Malevolence*, dodging heavy flak and the giant ship's weapon towers. But Shadow Squadron is running out of pilots—and of time!

2 As Shadow Squadron takes more losses, Anakin's pilots stay calm. They rely on their training to avoid panicking or growing angry at the death of troopers they've fought alongside for many battles.

3 The best tribute a pilot can possibly give a fallen squadron-mate is to fire a torpedo straight into the heart of Grievous's flagship, blasting his droids into metal splinters!

NALA SE

Clones are little more than numbers in budget statements to most of the Kamino cloners, but Nala Se is different: She seems to mourn each soldier injured in battle, and wants to heal him as best she can.

DIRE WARNING

Via holoscreen, Admiral Yularen warns Nala Se that the medical center is in grave danger and must be evacuated. But, with so many injured clones being healed by the thick fluid within bacta tanks, she is concerned that it will not be possible to move all the wounded in time.

KALIIDA SHOALS

CLONE TROOPERS INJURED during the fighting in the Outer Rim often wind up at the Kaliida Shoals medical center, where the Kaminoan Nala Se and her staff are treating more than 60,000 wounded clones.

BACTA FLOW REGULATORS AND MONITORS

INJURED CLONES IN BACTA TANKS

CLONE MEDICAL OFFICER

KALIIDA MEDCENTER

★ The Republic medcenter began the war as a derelict station that in better days served as a merchant hub in the Enarc system. The Republic bought it, refurbished it, and towed it to the fringes of the Kaliida Nebula near Naboo.

CONTROL HUB

REACTOR

ASSAULT ON MALEVOLENCE

1 Their squadron decimated, Anakin and Plo order the Y-wings to direct all fire at the starboard cannon!

2 Hammered by torpedoes, the mighty ion cannons of the *Malevolence* explode in twin bursts of flame!

3 As Grievous struggles to accept the ruin of his plans, three Jedi cruisers decant from hyperspace and race for the *Malevolence*, raking it with laserfire!

Y-wing bombers batter the *Malevolence*, hoping to end Grievous's reign of terror and regain the upper-hand in the war.

4 An enraged Grievous orders a retreat into space controlled by the Separatists. He knows the Republic will follow his crippled ship.

"A PLAN IS ONLY AS GOOD

AS THOSE WHO

LONDON, NEW YORK, MELBOURNE,
MUNICH, AND DELHI

For Dorling Kindersley
Project Editor Heather Scott
Senior Designers Jill Clark & Guy Harvey
Designer Hanna Ländin
Brand Manager Lisa Lanzarini
Publishing Manager Simon Beecroft
Category Publisher Alex Allan
Production Controller Amy Bennett
Production Editor Clare McLean

For Lucasfilm
Executive Editor Jonathan W. Rinzler
Art Director Troy Alders
Keeper of the Holocron Leland Chee
Director of Publishing Carol Roeder

DK would like to thank Nick Avery for design assistance,
Clare McLean and Peter Pawsey for color retouching,
and Lucasfilm Animation and Stacy Cheregotis for
providing final frames for upcoming episodes.

First published in the US in 2008 by
DK Publishing, 375 Hudson Street, New York, New York 10014

08 09 10 11 12 10 9 8 7 6 5 4 3 2 1

Copyright © 2008 Lucasfilm Ltd. and ™
Page design copyright © 2008 Dorling Kindersley Limited

All rights reserved under International and Pan-American Copyright
Conventions. No part of this publication may be reproduced, stored in
a retrieval system, or transmitted in any form or by any means,
electronic, mechanical, photocopying, recording, or otherwise, without
the prior written permission from the copyright owner.
Published in the UK by Dorling Kindersley Limited. A Penguin Company.

DK books are available at special discounts when purchased in bulk
for sales promotions, premiums, fund-raising, or educational use. For
details, contact: DK Publishing Special Markets, 375 Hudson Street,
New York, New York 10014. SpecialSales@dk.com

SD408—06/08
ISBN: 978-0-7566-4121-4

Color reproduction by Alta Image, UK
Printed and bound by Lake Book Manufacturing, USA

Discover more at
www.dk.com
www.starwars.com